Mia Juhl

Enter Mr Citrus Man

First published in 2021 by Salamander Street Ltd.,
[illegible imprint text]

Enter Mr Citrus Man © Mia Juhl, 2021

All rights reserved.

Application for performance and anything to be photographically should be
addressed to the agent, To Salamander Street. Application permission to perform
etc. The performance is prohibited, and no other photocopying or the stock in any
title evidence of the occupation without the author's prior written consent.

You may not copy, store, distribute, transmit, reproduce or otherwise make
available this publication (or any part of it) in any form, or by any means
including, without, digital format, no changed photocopying without prior
authorisation. Without the prior written permission of the publisher. Any person
personal... does any unauthorised act in relation to this publication or
liable to criminal prosecution and civil claims for damages.

ISBN 9781913630843

Printed and bound in Great Britain

10 9 8 7 6 5 4 3 2 1

Salamander Street

PLAYS

First published in 2020 by Salamander Street Ltd.
(info@salamanderstreet.com)

Enter Mr Citrus Man © Mia Juhl, 2020

ISBN: 9781913630843

Printed and bound in Great Britain

10 9 8 7 6 5 4 3 2 1

Characters

PAT

PETE

GABRIEL

MIKE

MORMOR

SCENE 1

We are in **PAT** *and* **PETE**'s *bathroom. It's small with plants everywhere and tiles on the walls. There's a toilet, a bathtub, a mirror cupboard, a sink and a crooked homemade table. There are moving boxes around, decoration, packs of noodles, toys, hats and sunglasses etc.* **PETE** *and* **PAT** *live there, so it has a homey feel to it. When they move around in the bathroom, it's in a coordinated effortless routine, like animals in a small cage. They know their bathroom in and out and know the most efficient ways of getting around.* **PETE** *is sitting on the floor drawing a picture,* **PAT** *is standing reading the bible.*

PAT: I think I've figured out the meaning of life! God created the whole wide world all by himself in seven days. But then after all that, he must have been sitting there all alone looking at all these wonderful things, drinking wine, trying to play UNO by himself, feeling very lonely. So, he made Adam to share all his creations with. SO! The meaning of life must be that we are meant to grow old together here in our little pocket, be something for someone and to share our creations with each other. TADAAA!

PETE: What creations?

PAT *thinks.*

PETE: We have our table. That's one creation

PAT: And we have a miracle! Is that a creation?

PETE: What do you mean?

PAT: Well, this planet has existed for billions of years and by chance, we ended up living at the same time, meeting each other and loving each other – that is our miracle

PETE: And THIS! *(Shows her his drawing.)*

PAT: What's that?

PETE: It's a drawing I made for you. Look, that's me, and there's you with your beautiful hair.

PAT: Perfect! We have figured out life then!

They dance a little happy dance.

PETE: We don't have to change ever!

PAT: What's that?

PETE: That's a dragon

PAT: Why is that there?

PETE: Uhm, I probably should tell you something

PAT: Something fun?

PETE: No

PAT: Then I would like to take it back please.

PETE: But I have been holding it in all day, and you know what we say

PAT: To never hold anything in cause it gives you a bad stomach.

PETE: Exactly, I just didn't know how to tell you

PAT: I don't know either, we can just talk about something else

PETE: But we need to

> **PAT** *moves as far away from* **PETE** *as possible.*

PETE: What's this now?

PAT: Do you know why they call it space?

PETE: Who are they? I think I call it space too? Or do I call it the universe?

PAT: RIGHT! So – SPACE! Space the name, not space the space. Is the actual WORD for space Isn't that incredible? Right now, there is space between us, and there is a space button that separates numbers and letters from each other, and in "space" there is just a lot of all that separation, so they have decided to call it space – because there is so much of it! And the more I think about this, the less space there is in my head! So the more I think about space, the less space there is. But I can't stop thinking about it. I want to write a book about it. S-P-A-C-E.

PETE: Stop all this distraction! It's now. I am putting my foot down. Now is the right time.

PAT: *(Sighs.)* What kind of hat do I need?

PETE: A serious one and sunglasses. I'll put on a fun hat to lighten the mood.

> *They both find hats and sunglasses and put them on.*

PETE: Are you ready?

PAT: YES to the hat, NO to the question.

PETE: Here it comes – someone has rented the rest of our home.

PAT: LIES

PETE: No, I'm not lying. That's one of our rules.

PAT: But you said someone had rented the rest of our "home", and it's not. We agreed on moving in here because we didn't like the smell in the other rooms, and the acoustic made me feel like I didn't exist. This right here is our home. Who is it? *(Starts angrily to water all the plants.)*

PETE: A man in a dragon shirt. He smelled of citrus. I don't remember his name, but he had green eyes, and I know you like green eyes, so I said yes.

PAT: I do like green. But I don't like any of the other things you said.

PETE: That he had a dragon shirt?

PAT: Yes. That is a danger signal, maybe he is dangerous, and does dangerous things that put us in danger, and we don't want that, DO WE?! Then he could just go out and rob a bank; that would maybe be less dangerous than having him moving in. We don't need his money

PETE: We do, though

PAT: Can we listen to the birds?

PETE: No Pat. This is a serious conversation and we need to end it before we can listen to the birds.

PAT: When does it end?

PETE: I don't know

PAT: Now?

PETE: NO

They both sit in silence for a little time, still in their hats and sunglasses.

PETE: Now it has ended – see that wasn't so hard. Which birds would you like to hear. *(He takes out a record player.)*

PAT: Swallows, they remind me of my mom and simpler times.

7

PETE *puts on a record with bird sounds.* **PAT** *goes to boil the kettle. They make tea in coordinated movements.*

PAT: I'm so happy I fell in love with you. I wasn't even looking, when I found you. That was probably why I fell. No one falls on purpose.

PETE: Maybe they do? We haven't been out for years. Maybe everyone falls now?

PAT: Then it must be summer.

PETE: Why?

PAT: Because people fall in love in the summer. And they love in the winter.

PETE: What do they do in spring then?

PAT: They clean so everything is ready for them to fall in love. You know how messy it gets, you drink more wine and dance around knocking things down.

PETE: Did you clean before you fell in love with me?

PAT: I don't remember anything I did before I fell in love with you.

PETE: Me neither.

PAT: I remember when we met. The sun was in my eyes and you came and blocked it, and asked me out for ice cream, and then we went to your secret spot in the forest.

PETE: And we came home with red cheeks, leaves in our hair and lots of mosquito bites.

PAT: And we folded paper boats until you said you had to go, otherwise you would miss your bus, and I said:

PETE: I already miss you.

PAT: My hair was electric for weeks.

PETE: I couldn't ride my bike for days, because I was so happy, I couldn't get my arms down.

PAT: I couldn't control my smile, I still can't when I'm with you.

PETE: Imagine, we haven't been away from each other since that day, with raised arms, electric hair and uncontrolled smiles. *(Hugs her.)*

Having Citrus Man move in is not going to change anything I promise. He is not dangerous.

PAT: Maybe we should make him something then?

PETE: Like a table?

PAT: Like a song.

PETE: How do you make a song?

PAT: You just make it up as you go – 1234!

PETE: 5!

They both make up the song on the spot.

"Dear Mr. Citrus Man
Do you have your own pot and pan
Because we don't have two sets

Dear Mr. Citrus Man
You can borrow our watering can
If you promise to give it back

Dear Mr. Citrus Man
Can we buy an electric fan
That we all can share

Dear Mr. Citrus Man
Maybe if you still have a nan
She could come and bring sweets

Then we would all be happy
And we would all have a great time
Oh uh oh
Yeah we would all be happy
And we would all have a great time yeah!

Welcooome!"

We hear loud noises coming from off stage.

PETE: What is that?!

PAT: I don't know!

The noise becomes louder.

PETE: I know what it is! Put on survival gear at my signal!

Makes a weird physical movement.

PAT: What's that?

PETE: THAT WAS MY SIGNAL!

PAT: I DON'T KNOW ANYTHING ANYMORE!

They both put on biking helmets and sunglasses. They jump terrified into the bathtub to hide. Slowly the door to the bathroom opens. A **MAN** *in a suit and bare feet comes in. He looks around, sits down on the ground in lotus position and starts meditating.* **PETE** *opens his eyes and sees him. He signals to* **PAT** *that she can stop surviving now. They both look at him.*

PAT: Is he real?

PETE: Nope, nobody can sit that still, someone must have placed him here.

PAT: He smells of citrus

The **MAN** *takes one deep breath and opens his eyes.*

GABRIEL: Hello Pat and Pete – I could sense this room needed some calming down, so I took care of that for you. My name is Gabriel and I'm the one moving in.

PETE: *(Whispers to* **PAT**.*)* He has his own name.

PAT: *(Whispers to* **PETE**.*)* Now!

They both turn to **GABRIEL** *and start singing half hearted. They try to change the lyrics to "Gabriel" but it doesn't really work.*

GABRIEL: What are you doing?

PETE: What?

PAT: It's a song

GABRIEL: Is it a winner-song? Would this song win Eurovision?

PETE: What?

GABRIEL: Is that the best you can do?

PAT: We put our hearts and souls into this song.

GABRIEL: Did you really? Because I didn't feel it. At all actually. BUT I think you can do much better. Next time start with –

PETE: Next time? Are you going to move in again?

PAT: Why would we make it again? We have tried and this is what it is.

PETE: Why would you confuse us like this?

PAT: Why would we be on a Europe mission, when we are so happy right here?

GABRIEL: You don't seem happy right now, you seem confused and sad.

PETE: Well when you weren't here, we were happy, now you have made us feel all these emotions

PAT: Let's just show Mr. Citrus Man how happy we are when he is not here.

They both put on a fake smile and start fake laughing.

PAT: Fun, jokes, bubbles, glitter, laughter

GABRIEL: Wow I'm so sorry, I didn't know you were this happy when I'm not here. But what are you so happy about?

PETE: *(Hostile.)* We are happy because we love each other and that is making us happier than anything else we have tried.

GABRIEL: What have you tried?

PAT: We have tried uhm, and also, but then we, but that wasn't really

PETE: So we uhm, instead I for example tried to uhm, but that

GABRIEL: You don't remember anything you've tried or done or wanted to do before you fell in love?

PETE: We don't need to.

PAT: We have something that most people look for their entire life by doing all kinds of things, we have that, so why try anything.

GABRIEL: "Why try anything"?

PETE: Have you ever been in love?

GABRIEL: No, I work as a highly successful life guru, I don't need to be in love. It's a distraction. I simply don't want to be in love.

They both gasp.

PAT: *(Whispers.)* It's so sad when you meet people, who haven't found a pocket to crawl into.

PETE: Typical, "I don't WANT to be in love" typical typical typical. Denial denial DENIAL.

GABRIEL: Why would I ever want to crawl into a pocket? That sounds awful.

PAT: Look around you right now. Does this look or feel or smell awful to you?

GABRIEL: Actually it does smell fantastic in here

PETE: It's because of our air freshener, we use it all the time. *(He pushes the air freshener multiple times. They all giggle. GABRIEL mocks them by giggling excessively, takes the air freshener and throws it away.)*

PAT: Where are you from?

GABRIEL: *(Dramatic.)* I'm from the big city with the dark houses, yellow windows and people who have got nothing better to do than go to cafés, kiss each other, eat late night snacks and then wobble home under the stars. It's pathetic.

PETE: Is it true that the city changes mood according to the sea's colour?

GABRIEL: What?

PETE: When the sea is black, everything needs to go really fast! It can also be deep blue, that means everyone in the city are dreaming. People are sat under clear skies, hanging out the windows with eyes half asleep and far away hangs a saxophone attached to the moon. The moon is always yellow when the sea is blue.

PAT: What happens when the sea is green?

PETE: Then you can walk on it

GABRIEL: What?! *(Takes a deep breath.)* Who has told you this?

PETE: My dad, he used to hang posters all over the city.

GABRIEL: A poster hanger. Cute. More like a liar. The city is tough, time is money, life is short. It's a jungle out there, where only the best survives, and I'm quite a big shot in the city.

PAT: What does a life guru do? *(Goes to make cereal with milk.)*

GABRIEL: I make people believe that they can do everything they want to in life.

PAT: Do you believe they can do everything in life?

GABRIEL: Of course. I don't just improve my clients, I transform them. You can become anything you set your mind to, if you work hard enough.

PETE: Lies. You can't jump two meters up in the air.

GABRIEL: Javier Sotomeyer, 1993. The world record in high jump. He jumped 2.45 meters up in the air. He won-

PETE: *(Interrupts.)* Three meters! I want to change it to three meters! You can't jump three meters up in the air.

GABRIEL: If you work with me you might.

PETE: I don't know what you are selling, but we are not interested.

PAT: Thanks but no thanks. We ain't buying.

GABRIEL: *(Frustrated.)* I'm not selling anything; I'm here to help you achieve your dreams.

PETE: I don't have any. I have a miracle, and that's all I need.

GABRIEL: A miracle? Can you walk on water?

PETE: When it's green I can

GABRIEL: Oh wow. *(GABRIEL takes a deep breath, takes the cereal from them, then holds them both around the shoulder.)* Okay guys, I see what this is, and it's totally fine. Don't be embarrassed that you live in your bathroom, it doesn't have to be this way. I say; Be like the lotus; trust in the light, grow through the dirt and believe in new beginnings.

PAT: *(Leans forward to* **PETE.***)* Is he okay?

PETE: *(Leans forward to* **PAT.***)* It's hard to tell –

GABRIEL: I'm fine! I can hear you, okay?

PAT: Woaw. That is quite cool. Can I get super hearing too?

GABRIEL: I don't have super hearing!

PAT: You haven't even realized! I've always wondered when you realize you are a mutant!

PETE: Me too! I occasionally snap my fingers, to see if fire comes out. You are so lucky

GABRIEL: I am lucky yes. Because I've worked hard. You are 100% responsible for everything you do in your life.

PETE: I've lost the keys I was meant to give you

PAT: How can I be responsible for Mrs. Sleepy Eye, down at the grocery store hitting the dogs?

GABRIEL: Have you stopped her?

PAT: No? It's not my business. I like it just where I am.

GABRIEL: Well SOMEONE has to stop her!

PETE: You could do it

GABRIEL: Yes, yes I could, and I will. I'll run there right away.

GABRIEL runs out. **PAT** *and* **PETE** *brushes their teeth.*

PAT: Nice guy

PETE: I don't like him

PAT: Me neither.

SCENE 2

PETE *crawls into the bathtub.* **PAT** *turns off the light. She sits down and talks to a plant:*

PAT: Why would I ever go down to the grocery store and tell Mrs. Sleepy Eye that she shouldn't hit dogs, when I'm so happy right here?

A letter comes flying in from above. She looks confused around and then at the letter. She goes and picks it up. On the front, it says "TO YOU" – she opens it. It says; YOU ARE THE CHOSEN ONE. Now she really looks at where it came from and is even more confused, which turns into franticness. She folds it really small and digs it into the soil of one of the plants. She puts on the bird sounds really loud.

SCENE 3

PETE: SOMETHING IS WRONG

PAT: NO

PETE: WHAT?

PAT: NEVER BEEN HAPPIER

PETE: WHAT?

PAT: YES

PETE: TURN DOWN THE BIRDS

PAT: WHAT?

She turns off the birds.

PETE: TURN DOWN THE Oh. I was saying that, but then you did it and then…that was embarrassing. I don't like yelling without a reason, my dad used to always…

PAT: Where's the tea?

Looks for tea.

PETE: Oh no…WE ARE OUT OF TEA.

PAT: I knew it would happen! I told you this would happen

PETE: It's not my fault!

PAT: Who's fault is it then?

PETE: Yours?

PAT: No! Somebody else!

PETE: The universe?

PAT: Too big!

PETE: Your grandmother?

PAT: Too close

PETE: THE TEA!

PAT: YES! Of course! The TEA!

PETE: *(Self-satisfied.)* Mystery solved by detective Pete

PAT: *(Hostile.)* I might die if I don't get it.

They both end up standing confused facing the door.

PAT: Why are we both standing staring into the door?

PETE: We are staring into the door, because we don't know what to do.

PAT: Are you considering going outside?

PETE: Maybe

PAT: Remember last time?

PETE: Yes

PAT: When you put on all our survival gear, and you didn't make it more than a five steps down the stairs before you went into a glitch and yelled:" SOMETHING FISHY IS GOING ON" and you got eczema and had to lie down for two weeks.

PETE: Maybe the neighbours have some, and I'll ask them.

PAT: You are so brave! Here! *(She gives him survival gear. The mood turns very heroic, like a soldier going into battle.)* I wish you all the best of luck on your quest.

PETE: Thank you.

PAT: Come back really really soon!

PETE: I promise

PAT: And be careful

PETE: I can't promise anything

> **PETE** *leaves.* **PAT** *tries to convince herself that she is fine, but eventually cries. She notices that the plant is dying*

SCENE 4

PAT: Oh no no no no no no

> **GABRIEL** *enters.* **PAT** *doesn't notice him before he speaks.*

GABRIEL: When did you start?

PAT: Smoking?

GABRIEL: No, crying

PAT: I'm not crying. You're crying.

GABRIEL: No I'm not. I never cry. I have noticed your plant. It's dying

PAT: Yes thank you I know, can we talk about something else?

GABRIEL: What do you like to talk about?

PAT: Have you really never been in love?

GABRIEL: No. I've never had anything holding me back, and that's why I'm this successful and this handsome.

PAT: I once tried to make a table, but it would never stand because I forgot that it needs to have four legs to stand up. I kept only making three legs. Then one day Pete came by and helped me remember, and together we made this table. *(Points to the table.)* This table is my biggest accomplishment in my life, and I couldn't have done it without Pete.

GABRIEL: Is that table your biggest accomplishment in your entire life?

PAT: Maybe, I don't remember. Why does it matter so much?

GABRIEL: Because I don't believe you.

PAT: I'm happy!

GABRIEL: You are not happy

PAT: I am!

GABRIEL: I JUST saw you crying

PAT: Ups.

GABRIEL: Why were you crying?

PAT: Chopping onions

GABRIEL: I don't see any onions?

PAT: I poked myself in the eyes.

GABRIEL: Both of them at the same time?

PAT: Yes, to see if they were still there

GABRIEL: Look, I understand. It's difficult to deal with the fact that you are not happy, and you want more in life.

PAT: Is that why I cried?

GABRIEL: Yes, and now – Think really hard – There must be something you've always wanted to be.

PAT: *(Thinks.)* Beautiful – But Pete doesn't seem to mind. He thinks I'm beautiful. *(She keeps thinking. **GABRIEL** observes her.)*

Taller – I would like to be taller, so I can reach the highest shelves in the grocery store. But Pete always goes, so I don't need it.

GABRIEL: Think harder!

PAT: Can I be an animal? Because then I would like to be a bird. Because they can fly and oversee everything, and they have a nest, and they are fed bread, and they can sing. My mom used to sing for me. When I was little I wanted to be a singer.

GABRIEL: I KNEW IT!

PAT: *(PAT covers her mouth realizing what she has done.)* No no no no, I take it back!

GABRIEL: We have a goal! Come with me.

PAT: What? Out there? No!

GABRIEL: Yes! Come on, out of this room

PAT: I can't

GABRIEL: Of course you can. Look. *(GABRIEL goes and stands close to her. He holds her shoulders to calm her down. She is scared but fascinated by GABRIEL.)*

Repeat after me, *(Makes yoga inspired hand gestures)*: "I am amazing" – "I can do anything" – "I am prepared for success."

You feel it?

PAT: No.

GABRIEL: That's weird

PAT: Why?

GABRIEL: Cause you are the chosen one

PAT: What?

GABRIEL: You are the chosen one

PAT: How do you know about the letters?! I keep getting these-

GABRIEL: I know. And now I need you to come with me. We don't have much time!

PAT: No! Look, I'm happy. Life is simple. Stop making it not simple.

GABRIEL: Happiness is an illusion! *(Tries to hypnotise her.)* Something to keep you from doing what you were meant to do all along – come with me and change the world! *(Snaps his finger.)* And you're back in the room.

PAT: What? Change the world?! I can't do that!

GABRIEL: Of course you can. We don't have much time Pat. Come with me.

PAT: No no no, I'm not leaving my pocket. It could have dangerous consequences.

GABRIEL: Not as dangerous as staying here. The world is dying – do you really want to sit here knowing that you could have done something?

PAT: But I don't know what to do.

GABRIEL *is now half out the bathroom, holding his hand out luring her out.*

GABRIEL: Come with me – sometimes you have to listen to the signs

PAT *stands confused. He takes her hand and pulls her out of the bathroom.*

PAT: *(On her way out.)* HOW DO YOU KNOW ABOUT THE LETTERS?

SCENE 5

PETE *comes back home with a 100 boxes of chamomile tea. And puts them all in the bathtub.*

PETE: Are you hiding again? I must say this is much better than last time! I've missed you so much it almost hurt when I was away. Where are you?

He sees the dying plant.

Oh no, what happened to you? *(He sees the letter buried in the pot. He opens it. The letter is written with big letters. YOU ARE THE CHOSEN ONE.)*

What is this? Pat?

He looks around the bathroom and opens a box, in there he finds tons of letters with YOU ARE THE CHOSEN ONE written on it. He is very frightened and scared.

Mr. Citrus Man?

BLACK OUT.

SCENE 6

THE BIG CITY. There is a cold and hard and unsafe atmosphere, neon lights and the vibe of an alley in New York, or a Batman movie. Maybe even a fog machine.

PAT *enters the stage scared and uncomfortable. Like a fish out of water, she holds her breath and stays away from open spaces. She reacts to all the sounds of the city, clearly out of her comfort zone. She sees a man in the audience and stares for a long time.* **GABRIEL** *enters looking smarter than before, with a bluetooth earpiece, a to-go coffee, fake jewellery and sharp shoes.*

PAT: What's with that man? Why does he stand like that?

GABRIEL: It's because he is not attached to anything or anyone

PAT: Like you?

GABRIEL: No?

PAT: He looks so sad?

GABRIEL: Everyone is sad.

PAT: Is it autumn? People are sad in autumn. But don't mistake it for winter because a lot of people also get sad in the winter. They actually get depressed, which is ultra-sad. MEGA SAD.

GABRIEL: It has nothing to do with the weather. Actually, yesterday was quite nice. But it's winter inside people's heads.

PAT: They just need someone to come and change the weather for them.

GABRIEL: That is you. You are the chosen one.

PAT: WHAT DOES THAT EVEN MEAN?! I have never been chosen for anything before, and now I'm chosen for something I don't even know what is!

PAT looks confused and angry at **GABRIEL**, *trying to hold in all her emotions, she starts making the sound of "ohh no I'm about to cry and show emotions"*

GABRIEL: Ew, please don't cry. Take a deep breath with me, and remember our mantra.

Stands next to her and they do the yoga hand gestures together.

"I am amazing" – "I can do anything" – "I am prepared for success." Can we move on now please?

GABRIEL *snaps and* **MIKE** *comes in and puts a microphone mid stage. He leaves again.*

PAT: What's this? What's happening?

GABRIEL: Your first performance! The first step is always the hardest, but remember you are doing it for the world!

He starts pushing her with small pushes to the middle of the stage.

PAT: Uhm, AHHHH nononono! What if I fall???

GABRIEL: What if you fly? See it. Feel it. Be it. I believe in you. 1, 2, 3 and shine!

The lights turn to a spotlight on **PAT**. *She is standing mid stage in front of a microphone. She is trying to see the audience. She is very scared and confused.*

PAT: "I am amazing" – "I can do anything"

She sings.

"I once had four legs and arms
someone took me apart
And made you
I need to
Find you and become whole again
I need my best friend
It's you
I need to
Find
Now im lost
Fingers crossed
I'll be found
On the ground
And we'll be together
You'll change the weather
and make me happy
again.

And I'll never fall apart
I'll just go back to start
With you
I need to
Make everything go back in place

Fly out in space
With you
In blue
Lights
But I'm here
You're not near
On my own
Its unknown
But maybe I'll be fine
I'm done crying
And I'll be happy
Again."

Maybe the audience clap, maybe they don't. Whilst she's been singing, GABRIEL has been moved by her being, but tries to hide it.

PAT: *(Happy.)* Have I changed the world now?

GABRIEL: That song, did you just make

    PAT interrupts.

PAT: It feels like something has changed in me! I feel great! Like I feel my fingertips and look! everything is shaking. I feel like an earthquake. Maybe I HAVE changed the world

They both stand looking around in silence, waiting for a sign.

GABRIEL: I don't think so. You can't just save the world with one song, you have to keep on going.

She runs back to the microphone and starts singing something, but it doesn't work.

PAT: The mic doesn't work

A MAN comes out from the side.

MIKE: Did someone say Mike?

GABRIEL: Oh hey Mike! This is my friend Mike. Mike this is Pat. Pat say hi to Mike.

PAT: Hi Mike. Is this your mic?

MIKE: Yes it is my mic. I might have to take it. Nice song. If you keep on going, you might change the world some day!

MIKE *takes the mic and leaves.*

GABRIEL: Yes she will! Bye Mike! Thanks for the mic!

> **PAT** *is really happy. She is ecstatic! She realizes how much space there is in the BIG CITY.*

PAT: THERE IS SO MUCH SPAAAAAACE!

> **PAT** *runs around enjoying her new feeling, until she suddenly falls and hurts her hands.*

PAT: Aw…I can't change the world. I don't have the moves, or the tight jeans, or the cape,

GABRIEL: No no no no, you don't need all that! You have something very special. *(He takes her hands. They lock eyes with each other.)*

PAT: and I also don't have my Pete. *(She takes back her hands.)* and I can't leave him to save the world. So I'm sorry Citrus Man, I have to go home now.

> **PAT** *is sad, and bends her head as far as she can. She starts walking out.*

GABRIEL: But you have only just started. You can't give up already.

PAT: Don't follow me. Just go home.

GABRIEL: But, you have my keys…

> *They leave the same way out.*

SCENE 7

PETE *is running around in hat and sunglasses and is frantically trying to water the plants, talking to them and trying to calm them and himself down. There is a mess everywhere and there are letters spread around the bathroom.* **PAT** *enters.*

PETE: No no no no, please don't die. She'll come back, just wait a bit more.

> *He sees her. Gasps and hugs her the hardest he has ever hugged her.*

PETE: See!! *(Pointing at the plants.)* What did I say?! She would come back! *Looking at her.* She is back. You are back. You are right here. Right where you belong.

> *She says nothing.*

23

PETE: I've missed you so much! So much that I went to the 24/7 drug store and bought a magazine with horoscopes, so I could find out how you were.

It didn't help me that much, but at least it didn't say you were dead.

PAT: *(Calms him down.)* I've missed you too.

PETE: Where have you been?

PAT: I've found a new feeling. I felt like an earthquake. Look! *(Exaggerated shaking her hands.)* I had no control, but it didn't hurt. It actually made me smile and run slash jump.

PETE: Where have you been?

PAT: I did something.

PETE: What?

PAT: I sang a song from my heart in front of some people. Gabriel and Mike liked it. And maybe if I keep doing it, I'll change the world. ME – change the world with a song.

PETE: I uhm…change the world? Why?

PAT: Because I'm the chosen one. *(Shows him the letter.)*

PETE: Gabriel? Mr. Citrus Man! Is he the one who has started all this?

PAT: No or yes, but it's true! I'm chosen!

PETE: I knew I shouldn't have trusted him! Nobody can smell that strongly of citrus!

PAT: You don't understand! It felt incredible.

PETE: More incredible than this? *(He hugs her with all his love. And squishes her face.)*

PAT: *(With a squished face.)* A different kind of incredible.

PETE: You are just confused. It's just a phase. Tomorrow everything is forgotten. Everything is going to be alright. Everything is going to be alright.

PETE *can't catch his breath. He is confused.* **PAT** *helps him to sit in the bathtub. She starts going backwards.*

PETE: What are you doing?

PAT: I'm walking backwards

PETE: Why?

PAT: So I can go back in time, and not make you sad. Just admit it!

PETE: Admit what?

PAT: That I'm an idiot!

PETE: You're not.

PAT: ADMIT IT!

PETE: No

PAT: You have to!

PETE: It's okay. *(He indicates that she should sit next to him.)*

She sits down. They both glide into the bathtub with their feet hanging out.

PAT: I'm not going to change the world, for you. I'll stay here.

PETE: No, I just don't want to lose you.

PAT: You can't lose something you don't own.

PETE: I once lost a sweater that wasn't mine.

PAT: *(Doubting herself.)* Hmmmmmmmmm. But, We are meant to go hand in hand through life, right? You and me. And grow old together, that's the meaning of life remember?

PETE: Are you happy?

PAT: I'm happy and sad and every emotion in between right now. Maybe that makes me confused.

PETE: But the most important thing is that you are happy. So if you need to save the world to be that, I won't stop you.

PAT: But then you won't be happy… I'm staying. and I'll forget everything and nothing has changed.

PETE: The plants almost died when you left…I almost died. I'm so tired. I haven't slept for the entire time you were gone. If I had one wish, you'd stay forever, but either way, I love you all the same. *(He is sleepy and closes his eyes.)*

25

PAT: And if you ever became green or lost all parts of your body, and just were a beam of light, I would still love you. I'm so sorry for all this confusion… I think I understand why people fall on purpose now. Are you still there?

PETE: Always.

He lies down to sleep. The lights dim. She sits and looks at the plants for a while. Then she quietly goes up and knocks on the bathroom mirror cupboard. **PAT**'s *grandmother "Mormor" opens up the cupboard, which is filled with fairy lights and glitter. She lives there.* **MORMOR** *has disco sunglasses, heavy makeup, jewellery and curlers in her hair. She is smoking and holding a drink with an umbrella in it. In the background you can hear 70's disco music.*

SCENE 8

MORMOR: MY BABYYYYY! The apple of my eye! It's been so long!

PAT: Shhhhh! You need to keep it down. People are sleeping at this time.

MORMOR: Well, we can sleep when we get old! You want a drink? *(Pours* **PAT** *a drink.)*

PAT: No I need advice.

MORMOR: On what?

PAT: My life

MORMOR: Live it! Done. You want a drink? *(Offers the drink to* **PAT**. *She takes it.)*

PAT: I AM living it.

MORMOR: Well, that's new. What happened?

PAT: I found a feeling mormor

MORMOR: Oh! that can be exciting, but dangerous. What kind of feeling?

PAT: The earthquake one

MORMOR: OH THAT'S one of the most dangerous feelings of them all! *(She sprays something to wharf the feeling away.)* How did you find this feeling if I may ask?

PAT: I tried out a dream I had forgotten I had.

MORMOR: *(Surprised.)* To pluck oranges in the south of Italy? How was it?

PAT: No, that one is still forgotten. I'm going to save the world.

MORMOR: The world doesn't need saving, it needs destroying. It needs a plague. *(Disappears from the cupboard to get something.)*

PAT: Mormor! Can you please leave this plague thing

MORMOR: *(From the back of the cupboard.)* Less people, less fuzz.

PAT: We have talked about this. It's not a popular opinion.

MORMOR: *(She returns.)* In here it is. *(She cheers to the back. No one cheers back.)*

PAT: MORMOR! Please focus!

MORMOR: *(Pouring herself a new drink.)* I'm always focused honey. So save the world?

PAT: Yes! Gabriel and Mike think I could.

MORMOR: Well that all sounds absolutely fantastic. FINALLY, you are talking about something REAL. I remember when I found the earthquake feeling. It was 1974 and I was playing Mikado, *(Flipping mikado sticks out like a fan.)* for the first time with my dad. I was really good! I made it to the world championship in Beijing in 1981.

PAT: What happened then?

MORMOR: I didn't go. *(Throws all the mikado sticks out into the bathroom.)* I had to bury the feeling. Far far away.

PAT: Why did you bury it?

MORMOR: I had other, more important things inside me, that I needed to use all my energy and love on.

PAT: Like what?

MORMOR: Your mom.

PAT: I miss her.

MORMOR: Me too.

PAT: *(Picks up the sticks.)* The problem is I also have another feeling inside me. One that makes me feel like everything is perfect right where I am, and safe and warm and unconcerned about everything.

MORMOR: Love

PAT: I'm so confused.

MORMOR: It's like a water tap with two handles. A cold one and a warm one. If you turn both of them on at the same time on maximum strength, then all the water will blast out and hit the sink so hard it all splashes up in your face, especially if you have a spoon lying in your sink, then you are soaked. You need to balance the two, depending on what you need.

PAT: How do I know what I need?

MORMOR: I don't know – meditate? Isn't that what the young people do nowadays?

PAT: I don't know.

GABRIEL *appears in the front corner of the bathroom smoking a cigarette.*

GABRIEL: I think you should listen to your mormor Pat. Come with me and I promise we will change the world.

MORMOR: *(Flirty.)* Who is he?

PAT: That's Mr. Citrus Man – he's a guru

MORMOR: A guru! Oh wow – Like Dalai Lama?

GABRIEL: No like myself – 100% original

MORMOR: Uh I like him! You should go with him

PAT: But what about Pete?

MORMOR: Who was Pete again?

PAT: Do you never listen to anything I tell you?

MORMOR: Let's not bicker in front of Mr. guru man citrus

GABRIEL: Do you want to keep the world waiting?

MORMOR: Darling, you are not falling apart, you are just falling into something different. *(Flirty)* and rather stunning if you ask me. Ups I think I need to top up. *(She disappears in the mirror.)*

PAT: Mormor?

MORMOR: Byeeeee. *(Makes a "call me" sign to **GABRIEL**.)*

GABRIEL: Can we leave now?

PAT: No! Yes! No! Yes! Just a second! Or 10, no probably about 1000 seconds. I just have to…

> **PAT** *finds a post-it note and writes.*

PAT: I'm sorry. Ps. please don't let the plants die

> *She leaves the note and goes to **GABRIEL**, who turns out his cigarette and sprays citrus scented air freshener all around him. She leaves with **GABRIEL**.*

SCENE 9: THE DOWNFALL

We are back in THE BIG CITY.
PAT *is standing alone on the stage with the microphone. She sings:*

"You're my schistosoma mansoni worm
And we'll stay together for life
You're my schistosoma mansoni worm
And I'll be your linoleum wife

You're my schistosoma mansoni worm
And we'll stay together for life
You're my schistosoma mansoni worm
And I'll be your linoleum wife"

> *A table is pushed on stage with ash trays filled with cigarette buds, alcohol and paper boats. There's also a depression lamp on the table. The setting suggests that they have tried for a long time to reach the stars.* **GABRIEL** *has changed. He looks stressed and smokes frantically.*

GABRIEL: What are you singing about?

PAT: A worm.

GABRIEL: How do you know this?

PAT: My dad was a biologist, and my mom was a tiny beautiful butterfly

GABRIEL: A butterfly?

PAT: Yes, that's how they met. My dad caught her in his butterfly catcher – he kept her in a jar, but he forgot to make holes. It's really important that you make holes in jars.

GABRIEL: Where's your dad now? *(He lights up a cigarette.)*

PAT: He works in a souvenir shop in Latvia. The last thing he said to me was "I love you" and looked me directly in my forehead – so I decided to go to an eye doctor, maybe something was wrong with my eyes, you know.

GABRIEL: Mmm, I don't think so.

PAT: It really takes a long time to save the world... When does it start to happen?

GABRIEL: Soon

PAT: But nobody comes and listens

GABRIEL: *(Unenthusiastically.)* Just remember the mantra – you know, "I'm amazing" "I can do anything" "I'm positive" *(Lights another cigarette.)*

PAT: *(Confused.)* "Positivity is a choice"

GABRIEL: What?

PAT: You said it wrong

GABRIEL: Whatever, it's not working anyway is it.

PAT: Maybe I should just go home...

GABRIEL: NO! No no no *(Takes a deep breath.)* Pat...I need you. And you need me, right? It's going to be just fine! You are beautiful and you are the chosen one remember? So just do as I say, I'm the expert on success here.

PAT: It's like no handles are turned on anymore.

GABRIEL: *(Loses his temper.)* Don't get distracted! I've told you this a million times! Forget the handles! There is only one fountain now, with shining gold.

PAT: I just feel like I'm stuck. Last night I was just sat overthinking. There was nothing, there was nothing, there was nothing, there was nothing, there was nothing, there was nothing, there was nothing, THEN THERE WAS SOMETHING for a brief moment. *(Pause.)* Then there was nothing again.

GABRIEL: Can you just stop talking for one second while I try to think.

PAT: What do you need to think about?

GABRIEL: Just.

PAT: Are you not happy?

GABRIEL: NO I'M NOT HAPPY. You can't be happy all the time Pat!

PAT: Why not actually?

GABRIEL: Oh my god all these questions! Question here, and question there! Do you know how this is making me look?

PAT: What?

GABRIEL: I give up everything for you! And what do I get? QUESTIONS!

PAT: I'm sorry

GABRIEL: Why can't you just

PAT: What?

> **GABRIEL** *tries to find his words, but gets interrupted by* **MIKE** *entering.*

MIKE: I've put the mic out for you.

> **PAT** *sits at the table and stares into the depression lamp.*

GABRIEL: *(Awkwardly.)* Oh hey Mike! M-M-M Mike! New haircut?

> **GABRIEL**'s *phone rings. He lights up a cigarette.*

GABRIEL: Yup! *(Touches his earpiece.)* Hello who is this? Do I have to? 1 sec. I'll have to take this one, it's a world famous record label that is interested in you! You know, like last week.

To himself so **PAT** *and* **MIKE** *don't hear him.*

Yes, I've been satisfied with your service. Average. Agree.

> **GABRIEL** *walks out.* **PAT** *sits and looks into a solar lamp/depression lamp. She takes out a box of pills. It's child proofed. She struggles to get them open.* **MIKE** *comes and takes the pills.*

PAT: *(Agressive.)* GIVE THEM BACK!

MIKE opens them for her and gives them to her quickly.

PAT: Gabriel gave them to me. They make it sunny in my head.
I take more when it's difficult keeping the clouds away.
Gabriel says that if I'm ever in doubt, I should just take another pill

MIKE: In doubt about what?

PAT: *(Excited.)* Oh you don't know! I'm gonna save the world! I just don't know when. He hasn't told me when yet, but just wait and see! Soon millions of people will see me, and they will all like me. And then I'll tell them about mom and how good she was.

It's not easy saving the world, but these makes it alright. They make tomorrow alright. And I don't know for how long I have to stay out here. I need them. *(Suddenly very serious.)* I've started to become invisible, I say "Hi" to people, and they don't reply. Even the raindrops have stopped falling on me.

MIKE: I can see you

PAT: You are just saying that.

MIKE: No?

PAT makes big movements close to MIKE. MIKE just stands there.

PAT: SEE! You don't even react! I'm invisible!

MIKE: Are you alright?

PAT: Never been better. *(Smiles with dead eyes.)* Why haven't I saved the world yet?

MIKE: I don't know. I just put out the mic

PAT: But I'm the chosen one...

MIKE: Aren't we all, *(Awkwardly laughs.)* I keep getting these in my mailbox.

He takes out the same letter that PAT has.

PAT: My letter! How did you get this?

She rips it out of his hand. She is frantic.

MIKE: Gabriel? He gives them out to everybody.

PAT: WHAT?! WHY?!

MIKE: He works for them.

PAT: WHAT?! FOR WHO?!

MIKE: GetLuckyLottery.com – look their website is in the corner, there. *(He points at the letter.)* Is this why we are doing this?

  GABRIEL *comes in.* **PAT** *is in shock.*

GABRIEL: Sorry I just had to

PAT: YOU!! YOU LIED TO ME! ABOUT EVERYTHING?!

GABRIEL: What I don't understand

She runs and tackles him, She sits on top of him, while she is strangling him.

MIKE: I'll just go out and remove the mic…

  MIKE *leaves.*

GABRIEL: MIIIIIKE! STOOOP! STOP! STOP MEANS STOP PAT!

  PAT *stops. She runs to the other side of the room where she walks around like an angry lion in a cage. She is MEGA angry.* **GABRIEL** *fakes that he is out of breath. She shows him the letter.*

PAT: What is this?!

GABRIEL: Uhm I don't have my glasses…It's your letter? You are the

  GABRIEL *pretends his phone rings.*

GABRIEL: Oh hey!

PAT: End that call now

GABRIEL: It's really important

PAT: Now!

GABRIEL: I'm gonna have to call you back. *(He "hangs up".)* Happy now Pat? That was maybe the most important person in the world, who just called to say he wanted to book you to sing, and you just lost all of that.

PAT: What was his name?

GABRIEL: Mike. *(Pause.)* Frank – uhm Mike Frank

PAT: Mike Frank?

GABRIEL: Yes Pat, that's a name

PAT: No! You just made that up! *(She points to the little email address.)* This is not for me! This is for everyone, so that makes it for NO ONE! WHICH MAKES ALL THIS A LIE!

GABRIEL: Pat, calm down

PAT: ARE YOU EVEN A GURU?!

GABRIEL: YES! *(Pause.)* part time guru, part time GetLuckyLottery.com worker.

PAT: How many people have you helped achieve their dreams?!

GABRIEL: Thousands. *(Pause.)* Ten. *(Pause.)* None. I just wanted to help

PAT: I DIDN'T WANT HELP. I was fine just where I was.

GABRIEL: You had forgotten all about your dreams, you were stuck in your stupid pocket!

PAT: *(Gasps.)* Don't you DARE!

GABRIEL: Sorry! I didn't mean that.

PAT: YOU LIED TO ME! I'VE BEEN BLIND FOR WEEKS FROM STARING INTO THAT THING! *(Points to the depression lamp.)* WHY?!

GABRIEL: I just thought if I kept you here…

PAT: That sounds like all the kidnappers I've been warned about!

GABRIEL: It's not kidnapping, please do not-

PAT: That's what a kidnapper would say!

GABRIEL: I found a feeling Pat

PAT: No, you didn't

GABRIEL: I did

PAT: What kind of feeling?

GABRIEL: The big one, you know

PAT: NO I DON'T KNOW.

GABRIEL: The one that makes me feel like everything is perfect right where I am.

PAT: Why should I care?!

GABRIEL: Because it is YOU! *(Beat.)* It's you that makes me feel this feeling, and I couldn't risk that feeling leaving me.

PAT: *(Realizes.)* Love. You found love. You are in love with me.

GABRIEL: Yes…yes I am, I'm sorry, I couldn't help it. I fell.

It just happened – you wouldn't understand

It's just, I've never met anyone like you, who has so much love to give, and I just thought If I could help you achieve your dreams, you would maybe give me a little bit of your love…Cause I've never been loved before…

I just wanted to be able to be something for someone, and I thought that someone could be you

PAT: You don't know anything about me

GABRIEL: I know that your favourite colour is lilac, and you don't have any sense of direction. You smile every time you see an animal, you whisper to the dice, your granddad was a wizard and you scream every time a car honks.

PAT: It's not EVERY time

GABRIEL: It is

PAT: I need my pills

GABRIEL: They won't help

PAT: What?

GABRIEL: They're just vitamins

PAT: So you were right. Happiness isn't real.

This is clearly a difficult situation for both of them.

GABRIEL: I never meant to –

PAT: What do you want me to say?

GABRIEL: I want you to say that you'd stay with me. We can save –

35

PAT: The world doesn't need saving, it needs destroying, a plague!

GABRIEL: Pat, just

PAT: NO YOU CAN'T HAVE MY LOVE!

Just leave. I don't know you! Leave and never come back… Please.

Pause. **GABRIEL** *leaves.*

SCENE 10

MIKE *comes back with the mic.*

PAT: Do you have any glue Mike?

MIKE: No, why?

PAT: I feel like there is a hole in me

MIKE: Glue?

PAT: Why do we fall, Mike?

MIKE: Uneven ground most of the time

PAT: But why do we keep falling?

MIKE: It's the way it makes us feel I guess

PAT: But it hurts so much, all over me.

MIKE: *(Hesitant.)* It's because your tree hasn't been watered for a long time

PAT: What tree?

MIKE: The one that grows inside you, it's dying.

PAT: What do you mean?

MIKE: Uhm…You know, when you meet someone, not just anyone, but like a uhm…a special person I guess, something happens inside you, not really, but it feels uhm…special, maybe like falling and flying at the same time, but a bit… *(Thinks.)* It all happens in the heart, when it's right, that uhm…special feeling. It's like they sow a little seed in your heart, and every time they look at you, say great things, make you giggle or hold your hand…they water that seed, and it grows into a tree. Maybe you've sometimes felt like you've had butterflies flying around in your stomach, but that's just the tree growing. It's quite amazing to have a tree inside you, it makes it easier to stand on windy days and you always have something to lean on. Some trees can grow all the way into your fingertips and out into your toes, if they get enough water. But if they don't, the tree starts to die. It decomposes and it hurts a lot, all over…From every cell in your body, down to where it all started, in your heart. It can feel like you are going to die, and it gets hard to stand up and put on clothes, but one day the pain will stop, and your tree has become soil, and it's ready for a new seed to be sown by someone else… special. But you can never forget about your trees, even if you really want to, because their memories lie in the soil of your heart.

PAT: *(Realizes.)* Oh no, Pete… I HAVE TO GO. Thanks for everything Mike!

She runs off.

SCENE 11

The bathroom. All the plants have died and the lights are dark. There is no one in there. The post-it-note still hangs on the bathtub. She looks around and finds a fun hat she puts on. She looks very sad. Then she takes a record with seagull sounds and plays. She starts singing:

Dear birds can you hear me sing
Up above the rooftops you're hovering
How easy it would be
To just fly and be free
Only you and me

And birds, can you tell me why
You can lose a piece of the blue sky
Something you don't own,
It just came along
But now it's gone

Dear birds, I should've known better
I'd just hoped he'd waited for her

Dear birds, I should've known better
I just hope he doesn't regret her

She takes off her hat, and stands for a little. The door opens. **PETE** *stands there with a new hairstyle, holding a box of fresh green cress in cotton. She doesn't see him.*

Black.

CPSIA information can be obtained
at www.ICGtesting.com
Printed in the USA
LVHW040817260121
677513LV00006B/526

9 781913 630843